For Kayla Rose. May you shine like a star x – J.W.

For my two grandads,
Grandad Fair and Grandad Smith xx – B.M.S.

First published 2017 by Nosy Crow Ltd
The Crow's Nest, 14 Baden Place, Crosby Row
London SE1 1YW
www.nosycrow.com

ISBN 978 1 78800 068 0

Nosy Crow and associated logos are trademarks
and/or registered trademarks of Nosy Crow Ltd.

Text © Jeanne Willis 2017
Illustrations © Briony May Smith 2017

The rights of Jeanne Willis to be identified as the author and
Briony May Smith to be identified as the illustrator of this work has been asserted.

A CIP catalogue record for this book is available from the British Library.

Papers used by Nosy Crow are made from wood grown in sustainable forests.
Printed and bound in Slovenia.

1 3 5 7 9 8 6 4 2

# Stardust

Jeanne Willis

Illustrated by Briony May Smith

nosy crow

When I was small,
I wanted to be a star.

My sister was a star. Everybody said so.
But nobody said it to me.

Mum lost her wedding ring.
I looked for it everywhere but my sister found it.
Mum said she was a star and so did Dad.

Nana showed us how to knit.

The scarf I made for Grandad
was full of holes.

But the scarf my sister made for Nana wasn't.

"It's perfect. You little star!"
said Nana.

We entered the Fancy Dress Competition.

Grandad said my costume was amazing.
He said I might win. But . . .

...I didn't.

My sister won the star prize.

Grandad dried
my eyes.

Later, Grandad found me gazing up at the sky.
There were thousands of stars. I made a wish . . .

I wished I was a STAR.

And Grandad said, "You are!"
Then he told me this story.
"Once upon a time,
there was . . .

# NOTHING.

No sun. No moon. No world.

No trees. No creatures. Just darkness.

But then...

# BANG!

Twinkle, twinkle.

The first star was born.

Then another

and another

and another

until...

there were billions of stars that

were brilliant and beautiful.

And there were planets, too.

With moons and mountains.

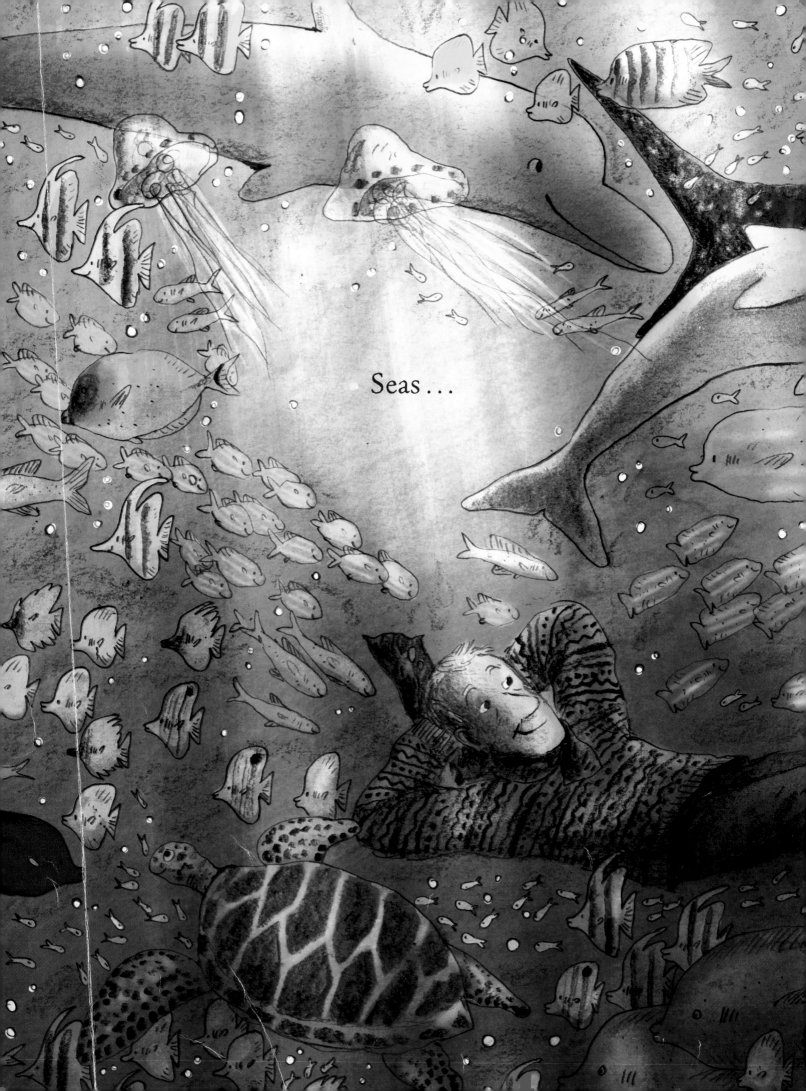

Seas . . .

and trees . . .

flowers and animals . . .
birds and butterflies . . .

BIG sisters and little sisters!"

"Everything and everyone is made of stardust,"
said Grandad. "That's why even the dullest
stones sparkle and shine after the rain."

"Will I ever sparkle?" I said.
"Will I ever shine?"

"You already do!" Grandad replied.
"Your sister isn't the only star in the universe.
Remember what you are made of . . .

you shine in different ways."

I did remember.

And I did shine.

Shine in your own way.

Because, remember . . .

. . . you are made of stardust, too.